THE MOUNTAIN OF A THOUSAND TOMORROWS

By Olanrewaju Idowu "Oladiamonds – The Strategist"

Copyright

Dedication

For everyone who has ever whispered,

"I'm tired,"

"I don't know what next to do,"

"I am confused,"

"What if …?"

and still showed up anyway.

For the ones who feel behind,

who scroll and compare,

who laugh on the outside

and ache on the inside.

You are not weak for feeling weary.

You are human.

This book is for you.

Author's Note

Dear Climber,

The world is moving fast.

News breaks every second.

Opinions flood your feed.

Everyone seems to be building something, launching something, becoming someone. And then there's you.

Maybe you're trying.

Maybe you're tired.

Maybe you're wondering when it will finally be your turn.

This book is not a list of rules.

It is not a perfect plan for your life.

It's a story.

A story about a girl named Kemi, who feels stuck while everyone else seems to be moving forward. A girl who receives a strange invitation to climb a mountain no one else can see. A girl who discovers that purpose isn't a destination you arrive at once, but a path you learn to walk, one honest step at a time.

As you read, I hope you see pieces of yourself:

- In her confusion

- In her comparison

- In her fear of not being "enough"

- And in her courage to keep going anyway

You don't have to have everything figured out this year.

Or next year.

Or even the one after that.

You just need to keep climbing.

This is my eternal gift to you,

It is borne out of my dark season experience,

I assure you that from the first Chapter of this book,

You will begin to climb again,

You will find deeper meaning you never thought existed in your journey.

With love,

Olanrewaju Idowu *Oladiamonds - The Strategist*

Table of Contents

Chapter One

The Invitation No One Sees

Chapter One

The Invitation No One Sees

The notification bar on Kemi's phone glowed like a tiny city at night.

New message.

New email.

New post.

New bad news.

She lay on her bed, the ceiling fan spinning lazily above her, the hum of her family's generator filling the quiet. The world outside still buzzed. The cars, the voices, the soft crackle of a neighbour's radio. But inside, Kemi felt heavy.

Another day of pretending she was fine.

She scrolled through her social media feed, thumb moving out of habit more than interest.

A classmate had just posted about getting a scholarship abroad.

Another was starting a small business.

Someone else had written, "New year, new goals, no time to waste."

Kemi's chest tightened.

She pressed her phone against her forehead and shut her eyes.

"What am I even doing with my life?" she whispered into the dark.

She is too old to be called a child. Too young to feel this tired. She had finished school, taken a gap year that stretched longer than she planned, and now… she was stuck between options that didn't feel like hers.

Her parents wanted her to study something "more serious" maybe nursing. Her friends talked about tech, travel overseas, content creation. Everyone had a direction, even if it wasn't perfect.

Everyone except her.

Her younger brother knocked lightly and pushed the door open.

"Aunty Kemi, Mum said to ask if you're eating."

"In a bit," she said, forcing a smile.

"You've been in here all day," he frowned.

"I'm okay," she lied. "Just tired."

He lingered for a second, then left, closing the door gently behind him.

The room felt smaller once he was gone.

Kemi rolled onto her side and grabbed the old notebook on her nightstand. It was the same one she'd carried since she was sixteen, filled with half-written poems, scattered goals, and to-do lists that never survived more than a week.

She flipped through the pages, hoping to feel some spark, some reminder that she once dreamt about things. Tucked near the back was a page she didn't recognise.

The paper was slightly thicker than the others, edges rough, as if it had been torn from another book entirely. A faint silver line ran around the border, catching what little light leaked in through her curtains.

Kemi frowned.

She hadn't glued anything in. And no one came into her room without knocking. Her parents were strict about that.

On the front of the page, in small, steady handwriting, were the words:

"To the one who feels stuck while everyone else moves.

There is a mountain waiting for you.

Not on any map.

Not on any app.

A mountain only those who are tired of pretending can see. If you are ready to stop performing and start becoming, your climb begins at midnight.

Stand where the sky feels closest.

Come with your questions.

Leave your perfect image behind."

At the bottom, almost hidden in the corner, was a single sentence, written so faintly Kemi had to hold the page close to read it:

"PS: Certainty is too heavy. Don't pack it."

She sat up. Her heart beats faster, not from fear, but from something else, something sharp and curious. "Who wrote this?" she whispered.

She flipped the page over. The back was blank, except for a tiny drawing of a mountain. It wasn't tall and dramatic, just a simple outline. But at the very top rested a small circle that looked like a sun… or maybe an open eye.

Kemi swallowed.

This had to be a prank. Maybe her brother. Maybe her best friend, Tayo. But neither of them had handwriting this neat.

And what did it mean, **"stand where the sky feels closest"**?

She checked the time on her phone. 11:42 p.m.

"If this is some kind of joke," she muttered, "it's a very weird one."

But something in her, the part that still believed in more than algorithms and deadlines wouldn't let the page go.

At 11:58, Kemi slipped on her slippers and tiptoed out of her room. The house was dim, her parents' bedroom door closed, her brother's soft snoring drifting down the hallway.

She climbed the narrow stairs that led to the flat roof of the house, where her mum hung clothes during the day and her father checked the water tank on weekends.

The air greeted her, cooler and lighter than it had felt all day. The city stretched out around her; rooftops, antennas, blinking lights, distant music. The sky above was wide and dark, scattered with stars that fought through pollution to be seen.

If anywhere felt close to the sky, it was here.

Kemi wrapped her arms around herself, notebook in hand. She checked the time again.

11:59 p.m.

"One minute," she whispered.

She felt foolish. What was she expecting? An angel? A shooting star? A voice from the clouds telling her exactly what to study, who to marry, where to move?

Still, she stayed.

When the clock on her phone quietly flipped to 12:00 a.m., nothing dramatic happened.

No thunder.

No lightning.

No voice calling her name.

Just the steady hum of the city and the soft beating of her own heart.

She let out a shaky laugh.

"Of course," she said. "Nothing."

But as she turned to go back downstairs, something caught her eye.

The page in her notebook was glowing, only softly, like moonlight on water. The drawing of the mountain shimmered, and the tiny circle at the top widened, like a pupil focusing.

Then, right beneath the original words, a new line appeared, ink swirling into existence as if written by invisible hands:

"You came. That is the first step."

Kemi froze.

Her breath hitched.

The rooftop seemed to tilt, the city blurring around her edges, not in a scary way, but like a camera shifting focus.

The mountain on the page grew larger, extending beyond the borders of the paper, lines stretching out until they were no longer drawings but something more, something real.

For a moment, she wasn't just standing on a flat roof in the middle of a noisy city. She was standing at the base of something tall, ancient, and alive.

A mountain.

Invisible to everyone else,

but not to her.

She gripped the notebook tighter.

"I… I don't understand," she whispered.

Another line appeared at the bottom of the page:

"You don't have to understand yet.

You just must be willing to climb."

Kemi looked up at the night sky, then back at the city.

Her life down there felt small and crowded. Full of expectations. Full of questions she avoided. But up here, holding this strange invitation, for the first time in a long time, she didn't feel behind.

She felt... called.

"I'm willing," she whispered into the dark. The page warmed in her hands, like it had been sitting in the sun. Then the glow faded. The mountain shrank back into simple lines.

The city returned to normal.

But Kemi knew something had changed.

The climb had begun.

What the Mountain Teaches

Not Every Calling Arrives Loudly

Most invitations do not announce themselves. They come quietly, often disguised as restlessness, dissatisfaction, or a question you can't shake. The mountain does not shout for attention; it waits to see who is listening. If you missed the noise everyone else heard, it may be because your path requires silence, not spectacle.

The Timeless Truths

- Some beginnings whisper because they need trust, not applause.

- If it keeps returning, it may be calling you forward.

The Climber's Creed

I don't have to see the whole way through,

to take the first small step I can do.

The mountain starts where I now stand,

With shaking heart and open hands.

The Fog of "I Don't Know"

Chapter Two

The Fog of "I Don't Know"

The next morning, the mountain felt like a dream.

Kemi woke to the smell of frying eggs and the sound of her mother's voice drifting from the kitchen, scolding someone on the phone about late payments. Her notebook lay beside her pillow, the page with the mountain neatly folded inside.

She opened it carefully.

No glow.

No new lines.

Just the same invitation, the same sketch, the same quiet words.

Had she imagined everything?

Her phone buzzed with notifications.

Her class group chat argued about several things, politics, life, career, business, the list never ends. Someone posted a motivational quote: "No excuses in 2026. If you're still broke, it's your fault."

Kemi rolled her eyes and locked the screen.

She got up, dressed, and joined her family in the sitting room. "Morning," she greeted, voice still heavy with sleep.

"Morning," her mum replied, eyes on her tablet. "Have you thought about what I said? Application deadlines are close. We cannot keep wasting time."

Her father nodded absentmindedly, scrolling through news headlines about rising prices, elections, floods in another part of the world.

Kemi picked at her breakfast.

"Yes, Mum," she said quietly.

"And?" her mother pressed.

Kemi hesitated.

And what?

And I still don't know what I want?

And I saw a magic mountain last night?

"I'm... still thinking," she managed.

Her mum sighed, setting her fork down. "Kemi, life won't wait for you to feel ready," she said. "When I was your age, . . ."

"I know, Mum," Kemi cut in, guilt prickling. "I'm trying."

Her mum softened. "I just don't want you to suffer," she said. "2026 is not like our time. Things are harder now."

Kemi wanted to say, That's exactly why I'm scared.

Instead, she nodded.

After breakfast, she escaped to her room. The noise of the house faded as she shut the door. She sat on the floor, back against the wall, notebook open.

"If this is real," she said softly, "what do I do now?"

The page did not glow.

No new instructions appeared.

She sighed, leaning her head back. A soft mist began to curl in the corners of her room. At first, she thought it was a trick of her eyes, a leftover from sleep. But it grew thicker, swirling gently like smoke without fire, cool and quiet.

In seconds, the walls disappeared behind a curtain of grey. She could still feel the floor under her legs, still hear the faint hum of the generator outside, but her room was gone.

She was sitting in the middle of a fog. "Okay," she whispered, heart racing. "This is new."

Her first instinct was to stand up and run. But where would she run to? Everywhere looked the same. Soft, shapeless, endless. A voice, neither male nor female, old nor young, floated through the mist.

"Welcome to the first part of the climb," it said. "The Fog of 'I Don't Know.'"

Kemi swallowed hard. "Who's there?"

No one stepped out of the mist. The voice seemed to come from everywhere at once.

"This is what it feels like when the future is blurry," it continued. "When everyone else seems to know and you don't. When every option feels both right and wrong."

"That sounds… accurate," Kemi muttered.

"You are not broken because you don't know," the voice said. "You are honest."

Kemi hugged her notebook to her chest.

"But what if I never figure it out?" she asked. "What if I keep choosing wrong things? My family and friends want answers. The world wants results. I'm tired of guessing."

The fog thickened, then thinned again, like it was breathing.

"Listen," the voice said.

At first, she heard nothing. Then, slowly, she began to notice sounds hidden in the grey.

The laugh of a child.

The flipping of pages.

The click of a keyboard.

The crackle of a microphone.

The sizzling of food on a stove.

The soft pluck of guitar strings.

Different lives. Different paths. Different futures.

"They all started here," the voice said. "In the fog."

Kemi frowned.

"How did they choose?"

"They didn't," the voice replied. "Not at first. They followed what pulled at them. What made them curious. What made time disappear."

Kemi thought of the things that made time vanish for her:

- Editing videos for friends

- Writing captions that felt like tiny poems

- Listening to people talk about how they felt, and secretly forming stories from their words

Nothing grand. Nothing that sounded like a "real career" when aunties asked at weddings.

"What if the things I like don't look serious enough?" she whispered.

The fog grew warmer.

"Who taught you that serious dreams cannot be soft?" the voice asked gently. "Who told you that what you love is not useful?"

Kemi had no answer.

In the distance, a faint outline appeared, tall and wide, reaching into a sky she couldn't fully see.

The mountain.

It was still far away, hidden behind layers of fog, but its presence was undeniable. Solid. Waiting.

"Every climb begins in 'I don't know,'" the voice said. "The goal is not to escape the fog. It is to keep moving through it."

"And what if I walk in the wrong direction?" Kemi asked.

There was a pause.

"Then you'll learn something you wouldn't have learned by standing still."

Kemi let those words settle in her chest. Maybe her problem wasn't that she didn't know. Maybe it was that she wanted guarantees before she took any step.

"And if I stop?" she asked quietly.

"You've already stopped," the voice replied. "That's why you were invited."

The fog began to thin. Her walls slowly reappeared, her shelf, her unmade bed, the clothes hanging on her chair. The notebook lay open in her lap.

On the page, a new sentence had formed beneath the mountain:

"Confusion is not failure.

It is the doorway to honest questions."

Kemi traced the words with her finger.

She still didn't have answers. She still didn't know what the next course to study is, what job to take, how to build a life that felt like hers.

But for the first time, she considered something new:

Maybe "I don't know" didn't mean she was stuck.

Maybe it meant she was on the first step.

What the Mountain Teaches

Clarity Is Not a Prerequisite for Movement

The fog is not a sign you are lost; it is a sign you are human. Waiting for certainty before moving often means never moving at all. The mountain allows fog not to confuse you, but to teach you how to walk without seeing the end.

The Timeless Truths

- You don't need the whole view to take the next step.

- Movement often creates clarity, not the other way around.

The Climbers' Creed

When all I see is cloudy air,

And every road leads everywhere,

I'll breathe, not rush to fill the space.

"I don't yet know" is still a place.

Chapter Three

The Valley of
Voices

Chapter Three

The Valley of Voices

Two weeks passed.

Life didn't pause for Kemi's mysterious mountain.

Her parents continued their gentle-but-firm pressure about life. Her friends kept moving. Some started online courses, others got internships, a few were already posting "First day at work!" selfies with smiling captions and tired eyes.

But the mountain was always there, just behind her daily routines, a quiet presence at the edge of her thoughts.

Every night, before sleep pulled her under, she opened the notebook. Sometimes new lines appeared; sometimes it was silent. Sometimes the mist returned, wrapping her in hazy lessons. Other times, she was left alone with only her questions and the sound of distant traffic.

One Saturday afternoon, her cousin Fola came to visit.

Fola was everything Kemi felt she wasn't; confident, focused, always five steps ahead. She had recently started a YouTube channel about productivity and purpose. People loved her.

"You just have to decide," Fola said, crossing her legs on the sofa. "The world won't wait. Pick something and commit."

Kemi tried to explain.

"It's not that simple," she said. "There are so many options. I don't want to disappoint Mum and Dad. I don't want to choose something just because everyone else is doing it."

Fola smiled, but her eyes held the kind of pity Kemi hated.

"Overthinking won't move you," she said. "You're smart, Kemi. You could be great at anything if you stop dragging your feet."

Kemi forced a laugh.

"Yeah. Maybe."

But the words settled on her shoulders like small stones.

That night, the mountain came again.

This time, Kemi didn't slip into mist while sitting in her room. She woke up already there standing in a wide, echoing valley at the foot of the mountain, the sky dim and crowded with clouds that looked like heavy thoughts.

Voices bounced off the rocky walls.

"You're wasting time."

"Other people your age already know."

"Are you sure this is practical?"

"That won't pay the bills."

"You're not trying hard enough."

"What if you fail?"

"What will people say?"

Kemi spun around, trying to find where they were coming from.

No one was there.

Just the voices, overlapping, rising, crashing.

"Hello?" she called. "Is someone there?"

Her own voice came back to her, slightly twisted:

"Is someone there… there… there…?"

The more she strained to listen, the louder the valley became.

It sounded like her mum.

Her father.

Her teachers.

Her friends.

People online.

Random strangers in comment sections.

It sounded like the whole world.

"Make it stop," Kemi whispered, pressing her hands over her ears.

"It won't stop," a gentle voice said behind her. "But you can learn which voices to turn down."

She turned.

For the first time, she wasn't alone.

Standing a few feet away was a tall figure. Not quite man, not quite woman. Their hair was threaded with silver, their clothes simple and earth-coloured. Their face was kind, and their eyes looked like they had seen many climbers come and go.

"Who are you?" Kemi asked.

"Call me whatever helps you listen," the figure said. "Guide. God. Spirit. Universe. Nature. Life, Voice-within. Friend. Echo-tamer. I've had many names."

Kemi raised an eyebrow despite herself.

"Echo-tamer?"

The figure smiled.

"The Valley of Voices is where most people turn around and go back home," they said. "The noise here is heavy. It convinces you you're late, foolish, selfish, unrealistic. If you don't learn how to walk through this valley, you will never truly climb your mountain."

Kemi swallowed.

"How do I walk through it?"

The figure pointed to the ground.

At her feet were two paths, both covered in stones.

The first path was wide and crowded with footprints. The stones on it were words etched in sharp letters:

"People's Expectations"

"What Will They Say?"

"Do the Safe Thing"

"Don't Disappoint Anyone"

"Be Like Them"

The second path was narrower, the stones more spaced out. The words on these ones were different:

"What Matters To Me?"

"What Do I Value?"

"What Kind of Life Feels True?"

"Who Do I Want to Become?"

"What Makes Me Happy?"

"What do I do that Make Time Passes so fast?"

"The voices on the wide path are loudest," the guide said.

"They are not all bad. Some come from love, others from fear. But if you let them be your only map, you will climb the wrong mountain and wonder why you feel empty at the top."

Kemi stared at the stones.

"So I should ignore everyone?"

"No," the guide said. **"You should *listen differently*."**

They bent down and picked up one of the wide-path stones. The words "Don't Disappoint Anyone" glowed faintly.

"This one is heavy because you're carrying it alone," they said. "Ask yourself: whose disappointment scares you the most? And why?"

Kemi thought of her mother's sigh. Her father's quiet, worried eyes.

"I don't want them to feel like they failed," she said softly. "They've sacrificed so much already."

The guide nodded.

"That is love," they said. "A good thing. But love gets twisted when fear is louder than trust. The question is not, 'How do I never disappoint them?' The better questions are, 'What kind of future would truly honour their sacrifices? What version of me will be able to give back, not just financially, but with a whole and honest life?'"

Kemi's throat tightened.

She had never thought about it that way.

The voices in the valley dipped for a moment, like they were listening too.

"And this path?" she asked, pointing to the narrow one.

"That is the path of your own questions," the guide replied. "It is not selfish to ask them. It is responsible. Every person whose life inspires you has walked this path at some point, even if they never talk about it."

The voices rose again, louder.

"You'll fail!"

"You're dreaming too big!"

"Who do you think you are?"

"You are not enough!"

"Others are more talented than you!"

Kemi winced.

"How do I walk when they're shouting?" she asked.

The guide placed a hand over her heart.

"Turn up this voice," they said. "The one that whispers when you're not performing for anyone. The one that knows what makes you feel alive even when nobody claps."

"What if that voice is wrong?" Kemi whispered.

"What if it isn't?" the guide replied.

The valley seemed to still for a moment.

A wind passed through, carrying away some of the noise. Not all of it, but enough that Kemi could hear herself think.

She took a step onto the narrower path.

The stone under her foot, *"What Matters To Me?"*, warmed slightly.

Then she took another step.

And another.

The voices behind her didn't disappear. They kept talking. Some shouted. Some pleaded. Some tried to guilt her back.

But with each step, she noticed something new.

Some of the voices cheered quietly:

"We just want you happy."

"We believe in you."

"We're scared, but we'll learn."

Love was in the valley too. It had just been buried under fear.

Kemi turned to the guide.

"Will this always be hard?" she asked.

"Sometimes," they answered honestly. "But once you know how to walk this valley, it becomes easier to visit without losing yourself."

"And what about you?" she asked. "Will I see you again?"

The guide smiled, eyes crinkling.

"Whenever the noise gets too loud," they said, "look for the questions that feel like truth. I live there."

The valley began to fade, walls dissolving, voices becoming echoes, echoes becoming memory.

Kemi woke up in her bed, heart still pounding.

On the open notebook beside her, new words had written themselves in soft ink:

Not every voice deserves a vote in your future.

Learn which ones to turn into background noise.

She exhaled slowly.

She was still scared.

But now she knew this: she didn't have to mute everyone, just choose who got to be on her inner volume control.

What the Mountain Teaches

Not Every Voice Deserves a Seat in Your Climb

Voices gather wherever uncertainty exists. Some mean well. Some are afraid. Some are simply loud. The mountain teaches discernment. Not every sound is guidance, and not every opinion carries wisdom.

Peace returns when you learn which voices to leave behind.

The Timeless Truths

- Volume does not equal truth.
- Protect your climb from borrowed fears.

The Climbers' Creed

Not every shout is meant for me,

Not every fear is prophecy.

I'll choose the voices that ring true,

And let the rest fade out of view.

I own the inner volume control.

The Cliff Called Comparison

Chapter Four

The Cliff Called Comparison

Sunday afternoons used to be Kemi's favourite.

Back in junior secondary school, she'd curl up with storybooks, eat rice straight from the pot when her mum wasn't looking, and dream about a future where everything just magically worked out.

Now, Sundays felt like report cards for her whole life.

After church, her parents napped. Her brother played games. Kemi sat on the sofa with her phone, scrolling through everyone else's achievements.

"New office, new beginning!"

"Finally entering my dream school!"

"Certified in three tech skills, no days off!"

She knew people only posted highlights. But highlights still hurt when your own life felt like a blooper reel.

She opened her notebook, half hoping the mountain would send some comforting line.

Nothing.

Only the same sketch, the same path leading upward.

"Fine," she muttered. "I'll come to you then."

The world shifted.

This time, there was no fog, no valley. Just a sudden rush of wind and the feeling of her stomach dropping, the way it does when an elevator moves too fast.

When everything settled, Kemi found herself standing on a narrow ledge carved into the side of the mountain.

The air was thin and sharp. The sky stretched out endlessly, streaked with soft blue and pale gold. Below, clouds swirled like oceans.

Directly in front of her was a cliff.

It wasn't smooth or flat. It was covered in glowing screens, tiny and huge, stacked and floating, each one showing a moving picture.

Kemi stepped closer.

The first screen showed a girl her age giving a TED-style talk, confident and polished, words flowing like water.

The next displayed a guy from her neighbourhood in a foreign city, wearing a winter coat, snow in his hair, captioned: *"We made it!"*

Another screen showed a friend who had started a clothing line. Orders flooded her comments.

Another display of a friend with her partner in a destination for holiday. Reels of romantic views of the landscape.

More screens. More lives.

Everyone climbing. Everyone rising. Everyone seeming to know exactly who they were and where they were going.

Kemi's breath shallowly caught in her chest.

"This is too much," she whispered.

"The Cliff of Comparison," a familiar voice said.

She turned. The guide stood beside her again, steady as ever.

"People spend years here, staring," they added. "Some never climb higher because their eyes are fixed on everyone else's path."

Kemi hugged herself.

"It's like my phone," she said quietly. "Except… bigger."

The guide nodded.

"Look closer," they urged.

Reluctantly, Kemi stepped nearer to the screens. On one, the successful speaker's perfect posture glitched for a second, revealing her trembling hands backstage. On another, the winter city blurred, and she noticed the boy's tired, red eyes when the camera turned away. On the clothing line page, beneath the smiling photos, Kemi could now see unsent messages, worries about rent, late-night tears.

The brightness dimmed, revealing the shadows.

"What you see is never the whole story," the guide said. "But your mind fills in the gaps with your worst fears about yourself."

Kemi swallowed.

"I know that," she said. "I say it. I repost quotes about it. But knowing doesn't stop me from feeling behind."

The guide's gaze softened.

"Behind what?" they asked. "Behind who? Did life hand out a schedule and forget to copy you?"

Kemi let out a weak laugh.

"It feels like it," she replied.

A gust of wind swept over the ledge, tugging at her black soft hair.

"See that?" the guide said.

On one of the screens, a girl sat on her bed, scrolling through her phone. Her face looked a little like Kemi's, tired eyes, pressed lips.

The girl was staring at a photo of someone else:

Kemi's cousin Fola, holding a plaque from her productivity brand.

Another screen showed someone watching a comedian, admiring their courage to be so open. Another showed a young boy replaying an interview with a nurse who'd saved lives during a flood.

"Everyone is looking up at someone," the guide said softly. "And many of the people you admire are looking up at others too, wondering if they are enough."

Kemi watched silently.

"But what about me?" she asked. "If I'm not as fast, or as loud, or as successful, what if I never catch up?"

The guide pointed behind her.

She turned.

There, carved into the mountain, was a long, narrow set of steps leading upward. Each step was labelled with words instead of numbers:

"Small skill"

"Quiet action"

"Tiny risk"

"Practice"

"Another attempt"

"Honest rest"

"One more try"

"Comparison shows you the finished pictures," the guide said.

"Your own path is made of steps, not screenshots."

Kemi stared at the steps.

"They look… boring," she admitted.

"They are," the guide said. **"But boring steps build breathtaking lives."**

The wind blew again, louder this time. The cliff of screens flickered, some images freezing, some repeating, some going blank.

"You can keep staring," the guide added gently. "Or you can climb your own steps. Both will cost you time. Only one will move you."

Kemi looked one last time at the screens.

At the scholarships. The visas. The studios. The shining faces. The awards.

Then she stepped away.

Her first foot landed on "Small skill."

Instantly, the nearest screen went blurry, as if someone had rubbed the image with their thumb.

She took another step.

"Quiet action."

More screens faded, their colours dulling.

By the time she reached "Tiny risk," the cliff behind her was no longer blinding. The images were still there, but they no longer reached into her chest and squeezed.

"I'll always see them, won't I?" she said.

"Yes," the guide answered. "But you don't have to measure your worth with them."

Kemi climbed, one slow step at a time, until the cliff sank below a layer of cloud.

When she woke in her room, her phone was on her chest, still open to social media.

She closed the app before the next video could start.

On the notebook page, beneath the mountain, a new line had appeared:

Their highlight is not your deadline.

Your pace is allowed to be human.

Kemi exhaled.

For the first time on a Sunday afternoon, she put her phone away on purpose and reached for a pen instead.

What the Mountain Teaches

Looking Sideways Weakens the Legs

Comparison pulls your attention away from your footing. When you measure your pace against another's path, you forget that terrain is never the same.

The mountain doesn't reward speed; it rewards steadiness and presence.

The Timeless Truths

- Their timeline is not evidence against yours.
- Balance is lost when the eyes stop looking forward.

The Climbers' Creed

I'm not too late, I'm not behind,

My path is stitched to my own time.

Their story isn't proof I've failed,

It is a testament that I can succeed.

My steps are mine, not for sale.

The Resting Stone

Chapter Five

The Resting Stone

The next few weeks, Kemi tried something different.

Instead of waiting to "figure out everything," she picked one small skill to practice: writing short pieces about feelings and everyday life, the way she wished people would talk about them.

She didn't post them anywhere yet. She just wrote.

Some days, the words flowed. Other days, her mind felt like wet cement.

On top of that, she helped at home, did errands, juggled family expectations, tried to stay updated with the world's chaos, and wondered, at least once a day, if she was already falling behind again.

One Tuesday, after a long day of chores and mental overthinking, Kemi collapsed onto her bed, still in her outside clothes.

She didn't even have the energy to reach for her notebook.

"I'm tired," she sighed into her pillow. "I'm tired of trying. I'm tired of thinking. I'm tired of caring and not seeing results."

She closed her eyes.

And slipped straight onto the mountain.

She stood on a narrow path, high above clouds that looked like spilled milk. The air was cool, the sky soft purple. But her legs ached as if she had truly been walking for days.

"Why am I this tired?" she muttered.

The path widened ahead, opening into a small, flat clearing in the rock. In the centre of it was a stone, not jagged, but smooth and flat, like a giant bench carved by time itself.

It glowed warmly, like it had been touched by sunlight even in the shade.

"The Resting Stone," the guide said, appearing beside her as if they'd been there all along.

Kemi frowned.

"I haven't done enough to deserve rest," she replied instinctively.

The guide raised an eyebrow.

"Who told you rest is something you *earn* by almost destroying yourself?"

Kemi looked away.

"It just feels wrong to stop," she said. "People are working harder than ever. The economy is a mess. The world is on fire. How am I supposed to rest when I haven't even achieved anything yet?"

The guide walked to the stone and sat down. The rock seemed to adjust under their weight, accommodating them like a cushion.

"Sit," they said.

"I'm fine," Kemi answered.

Her legs shook slightly.

The guide simply waited.

After a few moments, Kemi gave in and lowered herself onto the stone.

The moment she sat, her body relaxed in a way she hadn't realised it needed. The ache in her shoulders loosened. The tightness in her chest eased.

She hadn't known how heavy she felt until something offered to hold her.

"Rest is not a reward," the guide said quietly. "It is fuel. Even the healthiest body, the brightest mind, the strongest faith cannot run on empty."

"But what if I fall behind?" Kemi whispered.

"If your entire future depends on you never pausing," the guide replied, "then it was never safe to begin with."

Kemi looked down at her hands.

"I'm scared of being lazy," she admitted.

"So you swing to the other extreme," the guide said gently. "You try to outrun your fear by exhausting yourself. But exhaustion doesn't prove you're serious. It just proves you're human and ignoring it."

A soft breeze brushed over them, carrying the scent of rain and something like home.

"Do you know what 2026 has done to many hearts?" the guide continued. "Constant information. Constant crisis. Constant performance. The mountain is not taller than before, but people carry heavier loads while they climb."

Kemi nodded slowly.

She'd felt it: the weight of too many stories, too many expectations, too much noise.

"Rest on purpose," the guide said. "Not scrolling until your brain is numb. Not escaping from your life. Rest that returns you to yourself."

"What does that look like?" Kemi asked.

"For you?" the guide said. "Maybe it's journaling with no goal. Maybe it's lying on your back and watching the sky change colour. Maybe it's laughing with someone you don't have to impress. Maybe it's sleep. Real sleep. Not guilt-filled closing of eyes."

Thunder rumbled far away, soft and safe.

"But if I rest too long..." Kemi began.

The guide smiled.

"The Resting Stone is honest," they said. "It won't let you stay forever. The same way your body eventually wants to stretch after sitting, your purpose will nudge you to move again. Trust that."

They stood and offered Kemi a hand.

"Five more deep breaths," they said. "In. Out. Then you climb."

Kemi obeyed.

One breath for all the days she'd pushed herself without kindness.

One for all the nights she'd scrolled instead of truly resting.

One for the fear of being lazy.

One for the courage to pause.

And one for the strength to begin again.

When she opened her eyes, she was back in her room.

Her body still felt tired, but in a softer way, like after a good stretch.

On the notebook page, a new line had been written next to a small sketch of the Resting Stone:

You are not a machine.

Rest is part of the work, not a break from it.

Kemi turned off her data, put her phone face down, and let herself sleep for real.

What the Mountain Teaches

Rest Is Part of the Path, Not a Detour

The resting stone is not a failure point; it is an intentional one. The mountain was never meant to be climbed without pause. Strength grows not only in motion, but in stillness that allows the soul to catch up with the body.

The Timeless Truths

- Rest refuels what effort cannot sustain.

- Pausing does not erase progress.

The Climbers' Creed

I'm not a robot built to grind,

I'm bone and breath and heart and mind.

I'll lay my load down when I must,

So, when I rise, I rise with trust.

Chapter Six

The Mirror in the Wind

Chapter Six

The Mirror in the Wind

"Why do you always write about sad things?"

Tayo's message popped up on Kemi's screen one afternoon.

She'd sent her friend a few of her pieces, the ones about feeling stuck, about watching the world burn from a bedroom, about wanting to be useful and feeling small.

"Because people are sad," Kemi typed back.

"People are happy too," Tayo replied. "You're more than your worries, you know."

Kemi stared at the blinking cursor.

Was she?

That evening, she opened her notebook with a different kind of question in her chest:

"Who am I without my fears?"

The mountain didn't drag her in immediately this time. It waited, as if giving her a choice.

She closed her eyes.

"I want to see," she whispered. "Even if I'm scared of what I'll find."

The world shifted.

She stood on a high ridge, the wind rushing past her ears. The sky above was clear and bright. The path ahead was steep but visible.

In front of her, suspended in the air with no ropes or hooks, was a mirror. It wasn't made of glass. It rippled like water, surface shimmering with light and fragments of images.

"The Mirror in the Wind," the guide's voice said from somewhere behind her.

Kemi approached slowly.

At first, she saw her reflection as usual, the same brown skin, tired eyes, messy hair.

Then the wind picked up, tugging at the mirror's surface.

Her reflection shifted.

Now she saw herself at eight years old, sitting on the floor with crayons, drawing a whole city from imagination. Her eyes sparkled, tongue poking out slightly in concentration.

The wind blew again.

She was twelve, standing in front of her class, reading a story she'd written. Her hands trembled, but her voice was steady. Her classmates listened.

Another gust.

She was fifteen, comforting a friend whose parents were divorcing, listening more than speaking, offering tissues and quiet presence.

The images continued: little moments she had forgotten.

Times she had been creative, brave, kind, curious.

Times when she'd been more than confused, more than scared, more than stuck.

"These are fragments of you," the guide said, stepping beside her. "Pieces that got buried under anxiety and deadlines."

Kemi swallowed hard.

"They feel like someone else," she admitted.

"Because you stopped visiting them," the guide replied.

The mirror shifted again.

Now it showed the conversations she had with herself when nobody was around:

"You're so behind."

"Why can't you just get it together?"

"Look at your mates."

"You're always starting and not finishing."

Kemi winced.

"This is also you," the guide said, voice gentle. "Not the whole you, but a part that thinks it is protecting you by being cruel."

Tears pricked Kemi's eyes.

"I didn't realise I was this harsh," she whispered.

The mirror changed once more.

Now it showed shadows of possibilities. Kemi sitting in a small studio recording honest audio letters for people who felt lost, Kemi working with a team to create mental health content for young people, Kemi speaking softly in workshops, not as a loud motivational speaker, but as a truthful storyteller.

They weren't fixed futures, just outlines.

"Who you've been, who you tell yourself you are, and who you could be," the guide said. "All three live in you at once."

Kemi hugged herself.

"How do I know which one is real?" she asked.

"They all are," the guide answered. "But the one you feed most becomes the loudest."

The wind began to slow.

The mirror steadied, her present self coming back into focus. Not perfect. Not shining. Just real.

"What do you see?" the guide asked.

Kemi looked carefully.

"I see someone who... cares," she said slowly. "Someone who feels a lot. Someone who tries, even when she's scared. Someone who... maybe... wants to help other people feel less alone."

The guide's eyes softened.

"That," they said, "is closer to the truth than any insult you've used on yourself."

The mirror glowed faintly, then dissolved into the breeze, scattering like fragments of light across the ridge.

"If I forget again?" Kemi asked.

"You will," the guide replied. "But you can always return. Every act of honest reflection is another visit to this mirror."

Kemi nodded.

When she opened her eyes in her room, her face was damp with tears she hadn't noticed.

On the notebook page, next to a small sketch of a rippling mirror, was written:

You are not only what you fear about yourself.

There is more to you than your worst thoughts.

Kemi wrote beneath it, in her own handwriting:

"I am not just stuck. I am also someone who cares deeply and wants to tell the truth with kindness."

For once, she didn't immediately delete her own words.

What the Mountain Teaches

You Have Been Harder on Yourself Than Necessary

The mirror reveals what the wind has been trying to say all along, "you are not who your harshest thoughts describe". The mountain reflects growth you've overlooked and resilience you've dismissed.

Compassion sharpens vision more than criticism ever could.

The Timeless Truths

- Growth is happening, even when it feels slow.

- Speak to yourself as you would to someone you love.

The Climbers' Creed

I am not only all my flaws,

Not just the doubts that give me pause.

There's younger me and future too,

I'm many selves, all learning through.

The Broken Step

Chapter Seven

The Broken Step

Clarity is beautiful.

It is also fragile.

After the Mirror in the Wind, Kemi felt lighter. Not fixed, not suddenly sure of her life plan, but more… anchored.

So when an opportunity came, she decided to act.

Her church announced they were starting a small media team to create short videos and posts encouraging young people who struggled with anxiety, faith, and uncertainty about the future.

"Maybe this is it," Tayo said over a voice note. "You always write about feelings. You could help."

Kemi hesitated.

"What if I mess up?" she asked.

"Then you learn," Tayo replied. "They're asking for volunteers, not experts."

Kemi filled out the form.

The leader replied with excitement. "We've seen some of your writing," she said in a call. "We'd love for you to help with scripts and captions."

Kemi's heart soared.

She prayed. She planned. She scribbled ideas in her notebook. For the first time in a while, she felt like her small, quiet gift could touch someone else's life.

The first recording day arrived.

She wore her favourite shirt, packed her notebook, and went early. The team buzzed with energy, lights being adjusted, cameras checked, mics tested.

But as they began to film, things went wrong.

The camera kept malfunctioning.

The generator cut off twice.

Someone forgot a script at home.

And when it was finally Kemi's turn to share the piece she wrote… she froze.

The words tangled on her tongue. Her hands shook. Her voice wobbled. Halfway through, she lost her line and panicked.

"Let's start again," the leader said, encouraging.

But the more Kemi tried, the worse it got. Her mind went blank. Her heart raced. Her chest tightened.

After the fourth attempt, someone else was gently asked to read the script instead.

They did it in one take.

Kemi stood to the side, cheeks burning, wishing she could sink into the floor.

"Maybe writing isn't for me," she thought as she walked home slowly later. "Maybe I'm only good in my head."

That night, she didn't open her notebook.

She didn't want to see the mountain.

She didn't want another poetic line about growth or courage.

She just wanted to forget.

But the mountain did not forget her.

As she lay staring at the ceiling, the world slipped away.

She was back on the path, but something was wrong.

The step in front of her was cracked.

The word carved into it, "First Attempt" was split down the middle. A piece of the step had broken off completely, leaving a gap.

If she stepped forward, she could fall.

Kemi knelt to examine it.

"It broke because I'm not strong enough," she said bitterly.

"No," the guide's voice said behind her. "It broke because you used it."

The guide joined her, also kneeling.

"Untouched steps don't crack," they continued. "Only the ones that carried weight."

Kemi felt tears sting her eyes.

"It was embarrassing," she whispered. "I wanted to help. Instead, I made everything harder. They had to replace me."

"You were not replaced," the guide corrected. "You were adjusted for that moment. There is a difference."

"It feels the same," Kemi argued.

The guide gently touched the broken edge of the step.

"Tell me," They said, "what are you making this moment mean?"

Kemi swallowed.

"That I'm not ready. That I'm not good enough. That I should leave this work to people who can do it better."

"And what else could it mean?" the guide asked softly.

Kemi frowned.

"I don't know."

"Try," they insisted.

She took a deep breath.

"…That I need more practice," she said slowly. "That writing and speaking are not the same skill. That maybe I'm better behind the scenes than in front of the camera. Or… that fear still holds my throat when people are watching."

The guide nodded.

"Which of these meanings might move you forward instead of freezing you?" they asked.

Kemi thought about it.

"Needing more practice," she admitted. "And maybe accepting that I don't have to be good at everything at once."

The guide smiled.

"Failure is not a prophecy," they said. **"It's feedback.** The broken step is not the end of the path. It just tells you where reinforcement is needed."

They placed their hand flat on the cracked stone.

Light seeped from their fingertips, not erasing the crack, but filling it with a gold-like glow.

The step remained visibly broken, but now it was stronger than before.

"Climbers who never break a step often never leave the ground," the guide said. "You tried. You learned where you shake. That is precious information."

Kemi stood slowly.

"Will I feel this disappointed every time I try something new?" she asked.

"Probably," the guide said honestly. "But the disappointment will no longer be a wall. It will be a doorway you recognise: 'Ah, this is the part where my expectations and reality meet.'"

They gestured forward.

"Step."

Kemi hesitated.

"Even with the crack?" she whispered.

"Especially with the crack," the guide replied.

She inhaled and placed her foot on the glowing break.

It held.

Not because it was flawless, but because it had been seen, acknowledged, and strengthened.

When she woke up at home, the embarrassment hadn't vanished. But it no longer felt like proof she should quit everything forever.

She opened her notebook.

Under the sketch of a cracked step, the words read:

Your mistakes are not your identity.

They are maps showing where to grow next.

She wrote another line beneath it:

"Next time, maybe I'll let someone else speak while I write. Or maybe I'll practice speaking in smaller spaces first."

That night, planning felt like healing, not punishment.

What the Mountain Teaches

A Crack Does Not Mean Collapse

A broken step does not end the climb; it changes how you step next. The mountain teaches adaptability, not perfection. Falling is not the opposite of progress.

It is often the doorway to deeper awareness.

The Timeless Truths

- You are allowed to recover without rushing.

- What breaks can still support weight.

The Climbers' Creed

A broken step beneath my feet

Doesn't mean I must retreat.

I'll study where the crack began,

And strengthen there with gentler hands.

The Campfire of Questions

Chapter Eight

The Campfire of Questions

The mountain had mostly been Kemi, the guide, and the path.

She'd seen distant silhouettes of other climbers sometimes, tiny figures far away, moving at their own pace. But they always felt like background.

Until the night of the campfire.

It had been a hard day.

News notifications had piled up. Storms in one country, protests in another, job losses somewhere else, inflation rates, elections. Her aunt visited and gave a long speech about "serious careers" and "not wasting God-given potential."

Kemi smiled politely.

Inside, she felt like screaming.

That night, she opened her notebook almost angrily.

"If this mountain is real," she said out loud, "I don't want to climb it alone."

The world blurred.

When it cleared, she was in a wide, open space halfway up the mountain. A circle of stones formed a ring, and in the middle, a campfire burned, not orange, but blue and gold, flames licking the air without smoke.

Around the fire sat people.

Some older, some younger. Some in office clothes, some in hoodies, some in uniforms. Their faces were all turned toward the flames, eyes reflecting light and something else; tiredness, hope, fear, determination.

Kemi froze.

"This is… a lot of people," she whispered.

"They are all climbers," the guide said, appearing beside her. "Different mountains, similar weight."

A woman in medical scrubs hugged her knees, dark circles under her eyes. A young man with paint-splattered hands tapped his foot nervously. A girl in a hijab scrolled through her phone, then put it face down, as if it hurt to look at.

An older man with grey at his temples stared into the fire, lips moving silently with words he hadn't yet spoken.

"Sit," the guide said.

Kemi found an empty space on a log. The fire's warmth wrapped around her without burning.

No one spoke for a while.

The silence was not awkward. It felt like a blanket.

Finally, the woman in scrubs cleared her throat.

"I'm a nurse," she said. "People call me strong. They say I'm doing something important. But lately, I come home and sit in my car for twenty minutes because I don't know how to go inside. I'm tired of death. Tired of pretending nothing gets to me."

The fire flared gently.

"Why are you still climbing?" the man with grey hair asked her softly.

She thought for a moment.

"Because sometimes," she replied, voice breaking, "I see someone get better. And I remember why I started. And I still want to be there for one more person."

The fire glowed brighter.

The young man with paint on his hands spoke next.

"I'm an artist," he said. "My parents don't get it. Sometimes I don't either. The money is not steady. The world is unstable. It feels selfish to create when everything is burning."

"Why are you still climbing?" someone else asked, a woman with a laptop balanced on her knees.

"Because when I paint," he said slowly, "the noise in my head quiets. And sometimes, people see my work and say, 'That's how I feel, but I didn't know how to say it.' That... matters to me."

Around the fire, heads nodded.

One by one, they shared:

A teacher who loved her students but felt invisible.

A programmer building tools for people in rural areas.

A climate activist scared that nothing would change.

A content creator exhausted by algorithms.

A mother returning to school in her forties.

Each had doubts.

Each had questions.

And each, when asked, *"Why are you still climbing?"* found an answer that lived deeper than fear.

Kemi's turn came.

"What about you?" the girl in the hijab asked gently. "Why are you here?"

Kemi stared into the fire.

"I don't even know what my job is yet," she confessed. "I just… feel too much. I care about how lost people feel. I like turning heavy feelings into words that make people breathe easier. But I'm scared it's not useful enough. Not solid. Not… grownup."

The fire flickered.

"What happens when you don't use that gift?" asked the older man.

Kemi thought of all the nights she'd swallowed her words, all the times she'd stayed silent in group chats when someone confessed they were tired, all the drafts she never wrote.

"I feel… clogged," she said slowly. "Like I'm hoarding something that was meant to flow."

The group nodded.

"What if usefulness is not only about money or titles," the nurse said quietly. "What if usefulness is also about healing, even in small ways?"

"What if your voice keeps someone from giving up," the artist added. "Is that not useful?"

Kemi's throat tightened.

"I'm afraid," she admitted. "What if I'm not good enough to help anyone?"

The woman with the laptop smiled sadly.

"We're all afraid," she said. "We just choose what we'll do scared."

The fire flared again, sparks rising into the sky and dissolving into stars.

The guide stepped forward.

"This campfire appears whenever climbers forget they are not the only ones struggling," they said. "You are not a mistake crawling through life alone. You are part of a generation trying to build something human in a loud, fast, chaotic, demanding world."

Tears slipped down Kemi's cheeks. She wasn't the only one.

Not by far.

"Take something with you," the guide added. "A question from this fire."

Kemi closed her eyes.

One question rose above the rest, simple but strong:

"If I don't show up as myself, who will miss what only I could give?"

When she opened her eyes, the campfire had faded. Her room was quiet.

On the notebook page, beside a small drawing of a fire, the question was already written, waiting:

If you hide your honest self,

who loses something they didn't know they needed?

She didn't have an exact job title yet.

But she knew this: her life was not pointless. Her climb was not just for her.

What the Mountain Teaches

Growth Begins with Better Questions, Not Faster Answers

Around the fire, certainty softens. Questions create space for truth to emerge without pressure. The mountain honors curiosity because questions keep you open, humble, and moving in the right direction.

The Timeless Truths

- Asking well matters more than answering quickly.

- Wisdom often enters through uncertainty.

The Climbers' Creed

I'm not alone upon this height,

Others walk with flickering light.

We all are tired, we all are brave,

We show up so one heart is saved.

The Sky Shift

Chapter Nine

The Sky Shift

Something subtle began to change.

Not in the world. Headlines were still chaotic, the economy still shaky, people still rushing.

But inside Kemi, the sky shifted.

She started doing small, concrete things with what she was learning on the mountain.

She wrote short reflections and shared them anonymously on a small blog. Nothing fancy, simple text on simple backgrounds.

She volunteered again with the media team, but this time, she stayed behind the camera, helping with concepts, words, and feedback instead of forcing herself onto the stage.

She reached out privately when people posted vague, sad captions, sending messages like, *"I'm here if you ever want to talk. No pressure."*

She still didn't have a clear label for herself; writer, mental health advocate, storyteller, but she was moving. Gently. Honestly.

One evening, after she posted a short piece titled *"For The Ones Who Are Tired of Being Strong,"* she got a message from someone she didn't know.

"I don't usually comment," it said, "but this made me cry in a good way. I thought I was the only one feeling like this. Thank you."

Kemi stared at the screen, hand over her mouth.

Her words, her small, quiet words had crossed into someone else's night and turned on a light.

Later that night, the mountain came even before she opened her notebook.

She stood near the peak.

The path was still steep, but the air felt thinner, clearer. The clouds that had once crowded the horizon now lay below like seas of cotton.

From here, the view was wider.

She could see where she had come from, the Fog, the Valley, the Cliff, the Resting Stone, the Broken Step, the Campfire.

She could see other climbers at different points along their own paths.

"The Sky Shift," the guide said beside her. "The point where circumstances may still be confusing, but your perspective has changed."

Kemi took it in.

"I… still don't know everything," she said.

"You were never meant to," the guide replied.

"But I know this," she added, almost surprised as the words came. "I want my life to help people feel less alone. Whether I do that through writing, conversation, or creating spaces. I want to build calm in a noisy world."

The guide nodded.

"That is a direction," they said. "More powerful than a title."

The wind blew gently, carrying whispers.

Down below, a girl somewhere was reading Kemi's anonymous blog. A boy in another city was sharing one of her posts in a group chat. Someone was saving her words to read again later.

"You are already climbing, even when you feel like you're just taking notes," the guide said.

Kemi smiled faintly.

"But what if this changes?" she asked. "What if ten years from now, I want something else?"

The guide laughed softly.

"Then you'll climb differently," they said. "Purpose is not a prison. It is alive, like you."

They gestured toward the horizon.

"Look."

Kemi followed their gaze.

Far off, thousands of mountains rose, different shapes, heights, and paths. Some glowed faintly. Some were just shadows. People moved on all of them.

"The world told you there is only one right mountain," the guide said. "That if you don't find it quickly, you are lost forever. But in truth, purpose is less like a single point and more like a direction you walk in different ways over time."

Down in the "real world," Kemi was still figuring out school applications, budgets, family conversations. Nothing was magically easy.

But up here, seeing the bigger picture, she felt something new:

Permission.

Permission to start where she was, with what she had, and adjust as she grew.

On the notebook page, new words appeared:

You don't need a perfect plan to be purposeful.

You need a willing heart and honest next steps.

Kemi wrote beneath it:

"My next steps: keep learning about mental health, keep writing, explore fields where caring and communication meet."

The sky, both in her room and on the mountain, looked a little wider that night.

What the Mountain Teaches

Perspective Changes Before Circumstances Do

The sky does not change the mountain, but it changes how the mountain is seen. Sometimes nothing around you moves, yet everything within you does. The shift you need may already be happening above the noise.

The Timeless Truths

- A new view can unlock old terrain.

- Light arrives before relief is felt.

The Climbers' Creed

I may not see ten years ahead,

But I can light the step I tread.

Direction matters more than speed,

A faithful heart is what I need.

The Summit
Within

Chapter Ten

The Summit Within

The night the mountain took her to the summit, Kemi thought it was a mistake.

She had not "arrived" in normal life, not by any normal measure. Her parents still asked about school. She still woke up tired sometimes. She still compared herself occasionally, still doubted, still needed reminders.

But the mountain called anyway.

When the world around her faded, she found herself standing on a high, flat space at the very top.

The air was thin and crisp. The sky stretched in every direction, painted with early dawn colours, soft pink, gentle orange, pale blue.

There was no flag.

No trophy.

No cheering crowd.

Just silence. And vastness.

Kemi turned slowly, taking it all in.

"Is... this it?" she asked.

"For today," the guide answered, stepping out from behind a rock. "Summits are rarely final. They are just higher viewpoints."

Kemi walked to the edge, carefully.

From here, the world below looked small, cities, rivers, roads, tiny lines of light. She imagined all the lives being lived, all the questions being asked, all the mountains being climbed.

"I thought it would feel different," she said.

"How so?" the guide asked.

"I don't know," she shrugged. "Like I'd finally be certain of everything. No more doubt, no more fear. Just clarity and confidence forever."

The guide chuckled.

"Confidence isn't the absence of doubt," they said. "It's the decision to move with it."

They stood beside her.

"You came to this mountain because you were tired of pretending," they continued. "You felt lost, behind, unsure. You were carrying questions the world kept rushing you past."

Kemi nodded.

"And now?" they asked.

She thought for a moment.

"I'm still unsure about many things," she admitted. "But I'm not as ashamed of it. I'm learning to ask better questions. I'm more gentle with myself. I've started using what I have to help others, even in small ways."

She paused.

"And I know this: even if the world never claps for me, I want to live an honest life. Not a perfect one. A faithful one."

The guide's eyes shone.

"That," they said, "is a summit."

Kemi looked at them.

"Will I ever come back here?" she asked.

"You'll climb many summits," they replied. "Each one revealing another layer of who you are. But the mountain outside will matter less, because you'll recognise the mountain inside."

She frowned.

"The mountain… inside?"

The guide placed a hand lightly on her chest.

"Every question, every fear faced, every small courageous step, that is inner altitude," they said. "You came here to find purpose somewhere 'out there.' But what you truly found was your own heart. Your values. Your voice."

Kemi swallowed.

"So… what now?" she whispered.

"Now," the guide said, "you go down."

"Down?" she repeated, puzzled.

"Summits are not for staying," they replied. "They are for seeing. What you saw here? You carry it back into your everyday life, into conversations, decisions, work, rest."

They stepped back.

"The mountain won't trap you," they added. "It never wanted to. It only wanted to show you that even in a year like 2026, with all its noise and pressure, you can still walk in a way that feels true."

Kemi felt a mix of sadness and gratitude.

"I don't want to forget," she said.

"You will, sometimes," the guide said kindly. "That's why you have the notebook. The creeds. The lessons. The memories. And when the fog comes back, and it will, you'll know it's not the end. Just the beginning of another climb."

The wind rose around them, not harsh, just insistent.

Kemi took one last look at the view.

"Thank you," she whispered.

The guide bowed their head.

"Keep climbing, Kemi," they said. "Not to impress the world, but to honour the life you've been given."

Light swirled.

The summit faded.

She woke up in her bed, heart beating steadily.

The notebook lay open beside her.

On the final page of the mountain sketch, in large, steady letters, was written:

** The Mountain of a Thousand Tomorrows is not a place you visit once.

It is every day you choose honesty over performance,

courage over hiding,

and small faithful steps over fearful silence.

You are already climbing. **

Kemi smiled through tears.

She didn't have everything figured out.

But she no longer felt like a lost child waiting to be rescued.

She felt like a climber.

What the Mountain Teaches

The Peak Was Never the Point

The summit is quieter than expected. There is no applause, only understanding. The mountain reveals that the real ascent happened long before the top—inside patience learned, fear faced, and trust earned.

The Timeless Truths

- Becoming matters more than arriving.

- You were changing long before you noticed.

The Climbers' Creed

This is my climb, my one short life,

Through doubt and joy and dust and light.

I won't wait till I have it all,

To answer when my heart is called.

I'll walk when skies are bright or grey,

I'll rest, I'll rise, I'll lose, I'll pray.

And if tomorrow feels unknown,

I'll still move forward, step by stone.

The Mountain and You

Closing Chapter

The Mountain and You

Dear Climber,

You may not have a magical notebook.

You may never see a glowing mountain or a guide with silver-threaded hair.

Your path may look much more ordinary:

- a bus ride to a job you're still unsure about

- a classroom filled with faces and expectations

- a tiny apartment with bills stacked on the table

- a bedroom where your phone is both window and cage

But I hope, as you read Kemi's story, you felt something you couldn't quite name.

Maybe it was the sting of recognition.

Maybe it was the warmth of finally feeling seen.

Maybe it was a quiet voice inside saying, *"Oh… it's not just me."*

2026 is loud. 2027 will be louder. It may be another year or time that you are reading this.

The moment you get to this point in this book is YOUR YEAR. NOW IS!!!

There are wars and floods and injustice.

There are deadlines and data and DMs.

There are people telling you to "hustle harder" while your heart whispers that it's already exhausted.

In all of that, it's easy to believe life is only about surviving and performing better than others.

But you, Yes, you reading this right now, carry more inside you than survival and performance.

You carry questions.

You carry desires that don't always fit into neat career boxes.

You carry compassion, creativity, curiosity.

You carry a mountain.

Not a mountain of pressure.

Not a mountain of other people's demands.

A mountain of **tomorrows**, possibilities built from small, faithful choices today.

You don't have to move countries, launch a startup, or become famous for your life to matter.

You don't need a million followers to be impactful.

You are impactful when you:

- stay kind in a cynical world

- listen when someone is falling apart

- use your skills with integrity

- dare to rest so you can show up whole

- tell the truth gently, even when it costs you

- choose not to give up on yourself

- shine your light regardless

There will be fog again.

You will have days when you feel stuck, behind, confused.

When that happens, remember:

- The **Fog of "I Don't Know"** doesn't mean you're failing. It means you're honest.

- The **Valley of Voices** will always be loud. You get to decide who gets a microphone.

- The **Cliff of Comparison** will try to freeze you. Walk your own steps anyway.

- The **Resting Stone** is not weakness. It's wisdom.

- The **Broken Step** doesn't end the climb. It teaches you where to grow.

- The **Campfire of Questions** exists in every honest conversation—you are not the only one.

- The **Sky Shift** happens quietly, when you start acting in line with what you value.

- The **Summit** is not a finish line. It's a reminder that the real mountain is inside you.

You are allowed to change.

You are allowed to take time.

You are allowed to begin again, this month, this week, even today.

The climb is not about proving your worth.

You were already worthy.

The climb is about learning how to live from that worth.

I don't know all the details of your story.

But I believe this with all my heart:

The world is quieter, lonelier, and less bright without **your** honest presence in it.

So keep climbing.

Not perfectly. Not quickly. Just faithfully.

Step by step. Breath by breath. Tomorrow by tomorrow.

NOW is the tomorrow

I'll be here, somewhere on my own mountain, cheering you on.

With love from a fellow climber,

Olanrewaju Idowu "Oladiamonds – The Strategist"

If you want to share what resonates with you. Talk to me through climbers@peopleamp.io. I am doing collections of climber's notes to be published later. I will be looking forward to reading your notes.

Visit https://linktr.ee/peopleamp.io

My Mountain Affirmation

I am a climber, not a machine.

I am allowed to question, to pause, to begin again.

I don't need all the answers today.

I only need the courage to take my next honest step.

My pace is not a problem.

My story does not have to look like anyone else's.

I will listen for the quiet voice within me.

The one that values truth over performance,

kindness over perfection, progress over pressure.

I will not let comparison steal my joy.

I will not let fear decide my future.

I will not call myself names I would never call a friend.

When I fall, I will rise gently.

When I'm tired, I will rest on purpose.

When I feel alone, I will remember there are other climbers breathing beside me.

My life is not small.

My tomorrow is not hopeless.

My heart is capable of growth and courage.

I am here.

I am still climbing.

And that is enough.

"Still Climbing" – by Olanrewaju Idowu Oladiamonds

(*Soundtrack for* **The Mountain of a Thousand Tomorrows** book)

https://youtu.be/fU6EbWYqw0w

Verse 1

I woke up with the weight of yesterday
Too many voices tell me "hurry, don't delay"
Everybody running, I'm still finding my lane
Smiling for the world, but inside I feel the pain

Scrolling through the lights of other people's wins
Asking all my questions, hiding all my sins
But a quiet voice keeps calling me by name
Says, "You're not lost, you're just walking through the rain"

Pre-Chorus

I don't see the top, but I see my feet
One more breath, one more heartbeat
If the road is foggy, I'll walk it slow
I don't need it all, I just need to go

Chorus

I'm still climbing, even when the sky is grey
Still climbing, though I don't know the way
Every step is prayer, every fall's a lesson
Tomorrow's calling, I'm still pressing

I'm still climbing, not racing anyone
Still climbing, 'til my work is done
Mountain of a thousand tomorrows ahead
But today I rise, today I step

Verse 2

They say rest is weakness, but my soul needs air
I lay my load down, I find strength right there
I've broken some steps, yeah I almost turned back
But the cracks in the stone showed me where I lack

I met my fear, looked it straight in the face
Found grace in the pause, found hope in the space
I'm not behind, I'm right on time
This life is a rhythm, not a straight-line climb

Pre-Chorus 2

If I lose my way, I'll ask better questions
I'll listen to truth, not loud suggestions
If I fall tonight, I'll rise again
'Cause the climb itself is where I win

Chorus

I'm still climbing, even when the sky is grey
Still climbing, though I don't know the way
Every step is prayer, every fall's a lesson
Tomorrow's calling, I'm still pressing

I'm still climbing, not racing anyone
Still climbing, 'til my work is done
Mountain of a thousand tomorrows ahead
But today I rise, today I step

Bridge (Spoken / Sung)

I don't need perfection
I just need direction

I don't need the answers
I just need the courage

Fog don't mean I'm failing
Rest don't mean I'm weak
If I keep showing up
The mountain will speak

Final Chorus (Lift / Choir Feel)

I'm still climbing (oh I'm climbing)
Through the doubts, through the nights
Still climbing (still climbing)
Learning how to trust my light

Mountain of a thousand tomorrows ahead
But today I rise, today I step
I'm still climbing…
I'm still climbing…

Outro

One step
One breath
One honest tomorrow